I Never Said
I Wasn't Difficult

I NEVER SAID
I WASN'T DIFFICULT

Poems by Sara Holbrook

Boyds Mills Press

To my parents,
Suzi and Scott,
and to the Holbrook family,
for teaching me that lack of knowing
is no excuse for lack of trying.

Wordsong
An Imprint of Boyds Mills Press, Inc.
A Highlights Company
815 Church Street
Honesdale, Pennsylvania 18431

www.boydsmillspress.com

Printed in China

Publisher Cataloging-in-Publication Data
Holbrook, Sara.
    I never said I wasn't difficult / by Sara Holbrook.—2nd ed.
Revised edition.
[48]p. ; cm.
Summary: A collection of poems about feelings.
ISBN 1-56397-639-0
1. Feelings—Juvenile Poetry. 2. Children's Poetry, American.
[1. Feelings—Poetry. 2. American poetry.] I. Title.
811.54.—dc20   1996   AC   CIP
Library of Congress Catalog Card Number 96-85181

Second edition, 1996
Book designed by Tim Gillner
Cover concept and photography by The Reuben Group
The text of this book is set in 12-point Sabon.

10

TABLE OF CONTENTS

THE STORM THAT WAS

Me?
I rolled in like a storm,
darkening the room,
ominously rumbling,
then erupting with a BOOM!

> I HATE PEOPLE.
> I HATE SCHOOL.
> I HATE WHAT'S HOT.
> I HATE WHAT'S COOL.
> I CAN'T STAND RIDING BUSES.
> ALL MY FRIENDS ARE MEAN.
> THE WORLD IS GUACAMOLE
>   AND
> I HATE THE COLOR GREEN.

And you?
You didn't run for cover
or have that much to say.
You listened to my cloudburst.

And the storm?
It blew away.

I NEVER SAID I WASN'T DIFFICULT

I never said I wasn't difficult,
I mostly want my way.
Sometimes I talk back or pout
and don't have much to say.

I've been known to yell, "So what,"
when I'm stepping out of bounds.
I want you there for me and yet,
I don't want you around.

I wish I had more privacy
and never had to be alone.
I want to run away.
I'm scared to leave my home.
I'm too tired to be responsible.
I wish that I were boss.
I want to blaze new trails.
I'm terrified that I'll get lost.

I wish an answer came
every time I asked you, "why?"
I wish you weren't a know-it-all.
Why do you question when I'm bored?
I won't be cross-examined.
I hate to be ignored.

I know,
I shuffle messages like cards,
some to show and some to hide.
But, if you think I'm hard to live with
you should try me on inside.

THE DUMBEST QUESTIONS

Of course,
I know where those shoes belong.
I guess,
I recognize that backpack.
And yes,
I pretty much remember
how to use a coat rack.

How come you're turning red?
Are you allergic to suggestions?
Chill.
Your temperature's on high,
you're boiling over with dumb questions.

Of course,
I know my name.
Yes,
I have ears and I can see.
It's just,
I wasn't sure
that you were spouting off at me.

MY SELF

My self conscious
   should keep quiet,
not stutter-stop-'n'-stammer.
My self conscious
   should sit still,
not jerk like a jumpin' jack hammer;
   tripping up the stairs,
   knocking over chairs,
   breaking out in swears,
   and collecting angry glares.

My self conscious shouldn't snort.
Definitely.
It shouldn't cause me pain.
It shouldn't laugh like a honking siren
or sweat like a tropical rain.

I'm tired of hearing this is normal
and that I'm going through a stage.
I want to set my real self free
and lock self conscious in a cage!

WRONG

I'd rather starve myself
or pay a million-dollar fine,
or serve a lengthy sentence
of the solitary kind.

I'd stay grounded from T.V.
for I don't care how long.
If I only had a choice.
I hate to say I'm wrong.

If I had a place to crawl,
I'd never come back out.
Then you wouldn't have to lecture
and I wouldn't have to shout.

I'd rather hide for life in dark
than face you in the light.
Because,
what's worse than being wrong is . . .
maybe
you were right.

TIME FOR RECESS?

I'd like an outdoor recess.
My inner moods
         swing,
they make
my mental hands
         wring
and poke my face into this pout.

Where's the bell?
I need to run
     and scream
         and shout.
I'm all tied up inside.
This is serious.

Let me out!

I HATE MY BODY

I hate my body,
I'm not going out.
I'll stay in this room
with my mouth in a pout
if I feel like it.
I couldn't care what you say.
It's embarrassing
to look this way.

My legs are too long.
My knees are like lumps.
My neck is too thin.
My face has these bumps.

My waist is too thick.
My eyelids are limp.
My nose is too big.
I walk like a chimp.

I won't go to school,
I'm beyond repair.
And what's even worse?
I have hopeless hair.

It's safer in here,
alone,
by myself.
Why couldn't I be
like everyone else?

A STEP

Two,
awkward about the front door
fiddling with good-bye.
Too close for a wave or a handshake.
Too close.
Too far.
Too shy.

A step in the dark . . .
Would it be an intrusion?
Would it ruin a friendship?
Cause conflict?
Confusion?

Two,
poised on that risky step,
not quite eye-to-eye,
searching for the right key
to get them through
good-bye.

ACCOUNTING FOR FRIENDS

Security
is a bank account
I keep inside my mind.
Friends can make deposits
to be returned in kind.

You like my smile?
My thoughts?
My heart?
I stash your words away,
and when I'm low,
I make withdrawals
to help me feel okay.

I like your honesty?
Ideas?
The choices that you make?
I say the words, contributing
to our friendly give-and-take.

Friendship — an investment,
where kindness is repaid,
accumulating interest
in trust for future trade.

LOVE GROWS

Not
priced and placed on shelves
or in windows at the mall.
Not
found cut-rate
at the drug store.
Not
available in "small."
Not catalogued.
Not readywear.
Not advertised.
Not slit to there.

Upstaging
fashion statements,
love doesn't speak,
it shows.
Love can't be manufactured.
It's a natural.
Love grows.

THE LONELIEST

I'm not going steady.
I'm nobody's best friend.
I guess I'm 'bout the loneliest
that anybody's been.

There's no one waiting at the door
at three for me to meet.
And if I'm late for lunch,
no one's saving me a seat.

My love life's not the topic
of hot homeroom conversation.
Like some old empty locker,
no one wants my combination.

This school's made up of partners,
two halves to every whole,
'cept me,
left on the outside,
like that clankin' old flagpole.

ALONE

Alone
doesn't have to be sad
like a lost-in-the-city dog.

Alone
doesn't have to be scary
like a vampire swirled in fog.

Alone
can be slices of quiet,
salami in between
a month of pushy hallways
and nights too tired to dream.

Alone
doesn't have to be
a scrimmage game with grief.
Alone
doesn't have to argue,
make excuses or compete.
Like having nothing due,
sometimes.
Alone
is a relief.

NEVER RESOLUTIONS

I'm NEVER getting married.
I don't think marriage works.
It's just people taking turns
at being designated jerks.

I'm NEVER having children,
whining makes me come unglued.
Babies make disgusting smells
and then they grow up rude.

If I NEVER couple up
or I NEVER kid-create,
then I'll NEVER have to share,
love and lose,
or hate.

Of course,
last month I swore
"I'm NEVER watching movies,"
after a sleepless scare,
and of course,
I changed my mind.
NEVERs kept
are rare.

HAPPY ALL AROUND

Happy settles,
an orange campfire in my chest,
peaceful.
Not a scattering wildfire
quickly covering ground.
A slow glow,
my inner circle,
warm,
attracting others all around.

LOSING IT

I must have lost a hundred pens.
I've lost my wallet.
I've lost my watch.
I can never find two slippers,
two sneakers or two socks.

I have a box of single gloves.
I've lost notebooks, papers, glasses.
I've lost pictures, sets of keys,
and two birthday movie passes.

I've lost stuff on the bus,
on my own, even on purpose.
I've lost soap and toys down the drain,
my copy of *Red Badge of Courage*.
I never have more than 51 cards —
so I am not discouraged.

If I can lose both my change and the movie
just walking home from the video mart,
then I can lose this case of hatred
that's strangling my heart.

COOPERATION

Cooperation's hard
and it's work
to make caring last.
Sometimes,
forgiveness is tough to chew
and understanding melts too fast.

I could always order it my way,
that's easy.
I could protect
me first and only.
I could never compromise.
But stubborn gets,
well,
lonely.

HAMMOCK TALK

I'm not stalled out in the dumpster
or burning rubber in over-drive.
No hungry school of piranhas
is nibbling me alive.
I'm separating myself
from the rest of the bees in the hive.

I'm not in the dark or in the way,
not stinging from anyone's pepper spray.
I'm comfortable, crashed
and tucked away
in my private stash of leftover day.
Hey! I double-checked my pulse,
the calendar, the time,
the sky is free of meteors.
I don't owe the world a dime.
I'm not frozen, boiled or crispy fried,
not starving, stressed, or scary-eyed.

I am s p r e a d o u t

like softened butter
and feeling . . . satisfied.

DEPRESSION

I used to think
depression
had to do with games.
And if I won one, it was gone.
And if I lost, it came.

Sometimes I cry for nothing.
Sometimes
bad feelings stick
tighter than Band-Aids.
Broken things can't all be fixed.

Anger makes my chest ache
when I can't say,
"I'm mad."
Sometimes
my outside's happy,
when my heart is feeling sad.

Sometimes
when I am leaving,
I wish I were coming back
but I have to keep on going
since my good-bye bags are packed.

Sometimes
I find depression
sneaks quietly inside,
then screams out
as some anger
or becomes
a place to hide.

ANGRY

You can't hold me,
  angry, angry.
When I'm angry,
  angry, angry.
There's no comfort
in your touching when I'm mad.

If you talk to me, I'll fight you.
If you reach for me, I'll bite you,
  'cause I'm angry,
  'cause I'm angry,
  'cause I'm mad.

Though at first
it wasn't you,
I was mad,
but not at you,
till you held me,
or you tried,
to push my mad aside.

I'm a raging storm inside.
You can't hold me
and you tried.
Now I'm angry 'cause you tried.

Now I'm angry with an anger
you can't hold and I can't hide.
  Angry, angry,
    angry, angry.
Can't control me,
    angry, angry.
You can't hold me
    angry, angry.
So don't try.

VIOLENCE HURTS

Flailing fists
can be one solution,
one way to conflict resolution.
So's an insult.
So's a gun.
We could fight to the death,
get vengeance obsessed,
or strike like a hit-and-run.

Or we could
huddle
on neutral ground,
pass a few words around.
For once,
we could see if just talking works.
Maybe settle this.

Violence hurts.

KIND?

Is it kind to be kind,
or am I a chump?
If I lend you a hand,
if I smile when you grump,
am I stupid?
A doormat?
A worm?
Or a fool?
Is it dumb to be kind?
Are selfish and cruel
always smart?
Weren't we born
with both
brains and a heart?

POPULAR

I'd probably be more popular
if I were always sweet.
No more moody roller coasters,
I'd be up and
not off-beat.
Considerate of others,
I'd be icing on their cakes,
a selfless, sugary confection
produced for all their sakes.

I could be a hot fudge sundae
and wear a cherry for a crown.
The world would gather with their spoons,

and I'd be nowhere to be found . . .

TO WIN

I really don't want to lose.
It's not
I've never lost before.
I did and did
and did,
and still came back
for more.

I know
that all good sports
learn how to win or lose
and not break stride.
That I can recycle pride.
That lost can play again.
That losing isn't a sin.

But . . . but
this time I want to win.

PRIVATE PROPERTY

It's my body,
my choice,
what food I put inside.
What I wrap around me.
What I show
and
what I hide.

I'm not a public trashcan,
a public road,
a public beach.
Public is for others.

Me?
I'm private property.

ATTENTION SEEKING

Is it just
that you're busy?
Working?
A loner?
Or rude.
Or is it really my fault
for your
long distance,
cold attitude?
Is it because you
are tough?
Or is it
I'm not good enough.

SPEAK UP!

Speak up.
Who you talking about?

Speak up.
It could be me!

Talking only takes two,
but gossiping really takes three . . .
Two people dishing it out
and the one they got cookin' about.

Gossip is antisocial,
not everyone gets a fair turn.
It sparks like a match in the trash
and more than one can get burned.

So.
Speak up.
Your whisp'ring's making me mad.
Besides,
if you're talking 'bout Chris?
I just might have something to add.

SCORING

You bet,
I got him back.

Just as bad
and more.

How could I just leave 'em?

Too bad,
I couldn't score
while I was getting
even.

ARE YOU THE ONE?

No games today, it's just into the bleachers
assembled for hearing our principal preachers—
No smoking.
No guns.
No drugs and
No fights.
No harassment of females.
No whites against blacks.
No blacks against whites.

Eyes rolled to the rafters,
half-listening through shoe-squeaks and pokes,
we slouch. Except for Priscilla,
and (naturally) she's taking notes.
Consequences:
Demerits.
Detentions.
Suspensions.

Outlined
by some names of those who have laid out
the maximum fine for flipping-off rules.
Those who've paid with their lives.
"Each year," they are telling us,
"somebody dies."

What a waste.
What a bore.
We couldn't care less.
What a joke.
We leave.
We laugh —
and we guess . . .

Are you the one?

SCREAM BLOODY MURDER

When I see bodies on the news
it makes me want to cry all night.
'Course even if I do
it doesn't bring them
back to life.

What's the use in caring?
Can't we just pretend?
That everyone is nice —
and that all lives have happy ends?

If I turn my back to horror
or hum and close my eyes.
If I just refuse to see,
does it mean
those wronged
die twice?

REMEMBER

I don't remember the first time,
how it started
or when.
But I remember
the night you brought me brownies
and said
it would never happen again.

I remember,
your hair was longer then
and your eyes swam over to mine.
I remember,
my smile stuck on my teeth.
I knew it wasn't the last time.

My eyes were sealed with tears
and it was hard for them to wake,
but that didn't seem to matter.
We hugged.
And the brownies tasted great.

GOOD GRIEF?

Grief gets worn out by grieving.
Pain's a coat I must put on
and wear around the house
till it no longer feels so wrong.
I can't leave it in the box
and claim it doesn't fit.
I can't bag it for the coat drive
or wait till I grow into it.
Not a color of my choosing
and nothing to brag about.
The sooner
I try grief on,
the sooner grief
will get worn out.

DIVIDED

We're not a unit anymore.
The family got divided.
When birthdays come,
I get two cakes,
but don't get too excited.

Two birthdays
can be kind of sad.
I'm learning to
subtract and add
faces to my party list.
Some are great
and others missed.

Birthdays didn't stop because
divorce divided up our hearts.
Now we party separately,
but get to multiply the parts.

NO

When I say I'd rather not
and you try to change my mind,
when I say that I don't want to
and you ask me
one more time . . .

When you tell me
that I have to
and I start to squint my eyes
in firm determination
and your volume
amplifies . . .

When you turn your voice to scream
because you think that works,
you're wrong.
I can turn my ears to numb.
Your yelling
makes my stubborn strong.

POUT

No use
acting nice to me
when I'm stuck
in a pout.
I can't let your
niceness in
until my mad
wears
out.

OPINIONS

When
your opinions
speak the loudest,
you expect
I feel the same.
But I'm not some
T.V. channel you can
reach across and change.

My views I choose
myself.
You want a change?
Change
something else.

DOUBT

Insecure
is a lace
untied
that in a race
trips me inside.

It hints
that I don't
have the stuff,
why try,
when I'm not good enough.
And once
I stumble
in my mind,
it's harder
not to fall behind.

It sure would be
a faster route,
if I could live
without a doubt.

SAFE INSIDE

The storm
blew into town
kicking hail up with its feet,
turning dust and dirt to mud
and puddles to iced tea.

The windows rattled in their sockets
but I didn't cry or hide.
You can watch a storm
and learn
when you are feeling safe
inside.